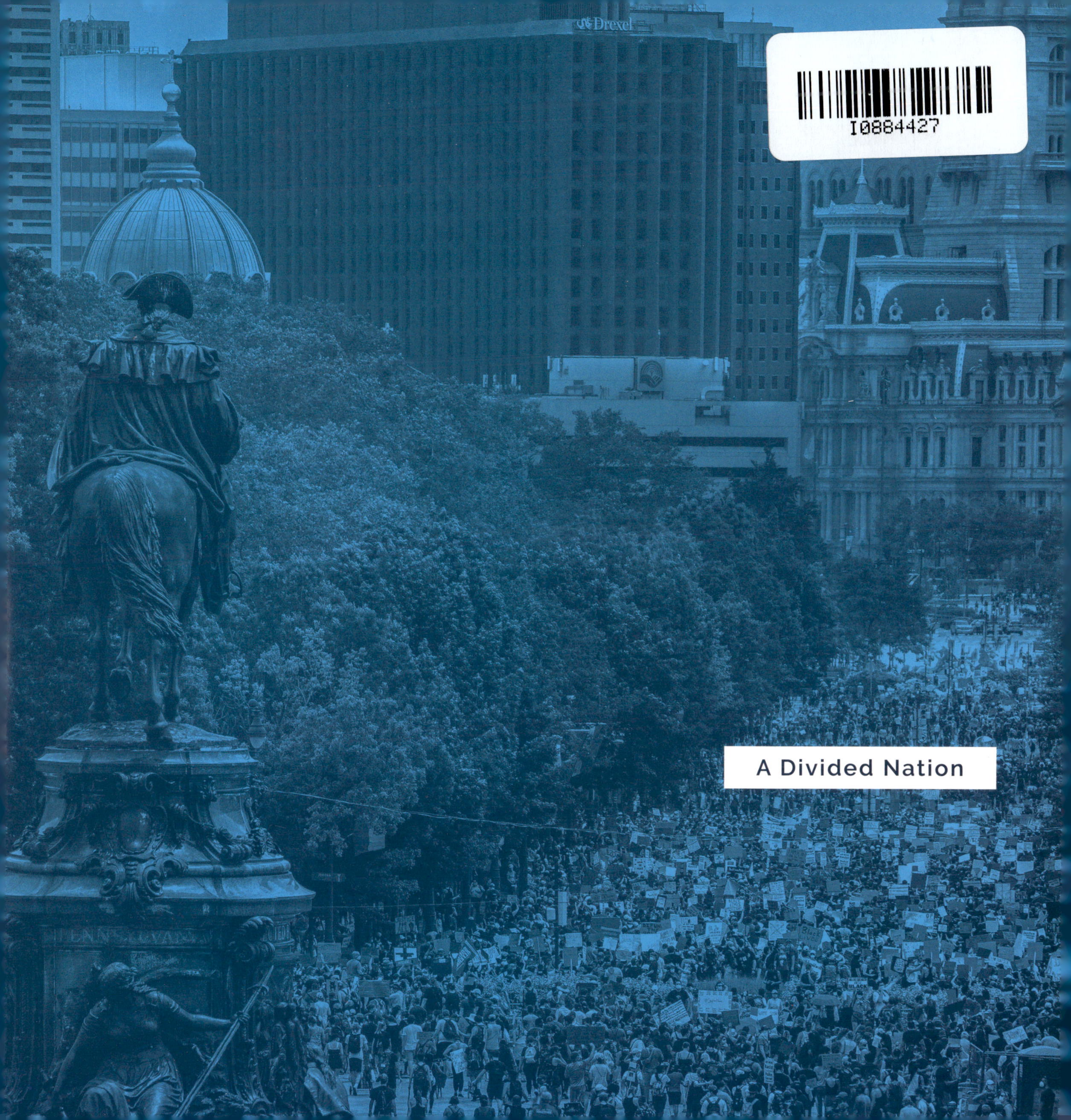

A Divided Nation

TRUMP
Trump
2020
KEEP AMERICA GREAT
TRUMP
2020
KEEP AMERICA
GREAT

A Divided Nation

Kremena Spengler

Living in AMERICA

CREATIVE EDUCATION

CREATIVE PAPERBACKS

Published by Creative Education and Creative Paperbacks
P.O. Box 227, Mankato, Minnesota 56002
Creative Education and Creative Paperbacks are imprints of The Creative Company
www.thecreativecompany.us

Book design by Graham Morgan (www.bluedes.com)
Art direction by Tom Morgan
Edited by Jill Kalz

Images by Getty (Aimee Dilger/SOPA Images, Anadolu, Bettmann, Brandon Bell, Graeme Sloan/Bloomberg, Hill Street Studios, Keystone Features, Nathan Howard, Santi Visalli, Universal History Archive), Pexels (Life Matters, Pixabay, Timur Weber, Trev Adams), Unsplash (Library of Congress, Tony Zhen), Wikimedia Commons (Angr, Howard Chandler Christy/The Indian Reporter, Matt Hrkac, Public Domain, Shaleah Craighead, Timothy H. O'Sullivan)

Library of Congress Cataloging-in-Publication Data
Names: Spengler, Kremena, author.
Title: A divided nation / by Kremena Spengler.
Description: Mankato, Minnesota : Creative Education, Creative Paperbacks, [2025] | Series: Living in America | Includes webography. | Includes bibliographical references and index. | Audience: Ages 12–15 | Audience: Grades 7–9 | Summary: "A social studies title for young adults that examines the history of division between Americans, focusing on the United States government and Democratic and Republican political parties. Includes sidebars, real-person profiles, a glossary, a timeline, and further resources"—Provided by publisher.
Identifiers: LCCN 2023046929 (print) | LCCN 2023046930 (ebook) | ISBN 9781640269064 (library binding) | ISBN 9781682774564 (paperback) | ISBN 9798889890744 (ebook)
Subjects: LCSH: Polarization (Social sciences)—Political aspects—United States. | Divided government—United States. | Political culture—United States. | Political participation—United States. | Party affiliation—United States. | Political parties—United States. | Right and left (Political science)—United States. | Identity politics—United States. | Social media—United States—History—21st century. | United States—Politics and government.
Classification: LCC JK1726 .S68 2025 (print) | LCC JK1726 (ebook) | DDC 306.20973—dc23/eng/20231214
LC record available at https://lccn.loc.gov/2023046929
LC ebook record available at https://lccn.loc.gov/2023046930

Printed in China

MP

Centre St
Chambers St
BLM
JUSTICE FOR
HOW MANY MURDERS

CONTENTS

FDR Dr
Pearl St
Park Row South
FDR Dr
North
BLACK LIVES MATTER
END POLICE BRUTALITY
George Floyd

Introduction

On May 25, 2020, a store clerk in Minneapolis, Minnesota, called the police. He said a Black man named George Floyd had tried to pay for cigarettes with a counterfeit $20 bill.

When officers arrived, Floyd was handcuffed. When Floyd resisted, officers pushed him to the ground, and a white police officer, Derek Chauvin, restrained him by pressing a knee to Floyd's neck. Chauvin held Floyd down for about nine minutes, despite Floyd gasping, "I can't breathe!" Floyd then died.

A bystander filmed the dramatic scene. The video went viral. Hundreds of protesters poured into the streets, demanding justice for Floyd. Police cars were vandalized. Businesses were looted and set on fire. The precinct where the officers served was burned down. Then U.S. president Donald Trump weighed in, calling the protesters "thugs," and adding, "When the looting starts, the shooting starts."

Protests spread to 140 cities across the United States. The National Guard was activated in 21 states. Floyd's family called for healing and peace.

Eventually, a report ruled Floyd's death a homicide. The officers were prosecuted, found guilty, and sentenced. The murder drew attention to police brutality against Blacks in the United States. It sparked calls for police reform and gave rise to the Black Lives Matter movement.

But not everyone felt the need for change. Some people saw the Black Lives Matter movement as divisive. They came up with the slogans "All Lives Matter" and "Blue Lives Matter" (in support of the police). The George Floyd murder revived the debate about race and put the nation's ever-deepening political divide in the spotlight.

LET THEM
BREATHE
BLACK
LIVES
MATTER
SYSTEMIC
#BLACKLIVESMATTER
RACISM IS A PANDEMIC
400+ INDIGENOUS DEATHS
IN CUSTODY
NO POLICE CONVICTION
ALL LIVES
DON'T MATTER
UNTIL BLACK
NO ONE
IS
ILLEGAL
ON
STOLEN
#solidarity

In 1787, the Founding Fathers of the United States signed the set of rules by which the new young nation would be governed.

CHAPTER 1:

Party History

Humans sort themselves into groups along a variety of lines. Race is only one of them. Others are gender, class, age, and political allegiance, to name just a few.

One way for people to promote their common interests is by forming political parties. These groups have their own ideas about the government's role and promote their own political goals.

The founders of the United States tried to avoid such disunity. Alexander Hamilton and James Madison wrote of the dangers of political division. In fact, the U.S. Constitution does not mention political parties at all.

Before the Constitution was **ratified** in 1787, the nation was governed under the Articles of Confederation. They gave almost all power to the individual states. The Constitution gave power to the federal government, including the president. The first political parties grew out of the debate about the Constitution. The people who wanted the Constitution ratified were called Federalists. They were the nation's first political party. The people who opposed ratification, and wanted the states to keep their powers, were the anti-Federalists, or Democratic-Republicans.

To get the Constitution ratified, the Federalists agreed to a Bill of Rights that included the 10th Amendment. This amendment said that all powers not specifically given to the federal government belong to the states. The debate about how much power the federal government should have is still going on today.

The Federalist victory in the ratification debate led to George Washington's election as the first president of the United States. In his famous 1796 Farewell Address, he warned against **partisanship**. Despite his advice, the first partisan election happened that same fall. Fellow Federalist John Adams defeated Democratic-Republican Thomas Jefferson to become president.

In 1800, Jefferson defeated Adams. This was the first transfer of power between U.S. political parties. The Federalists stood for a strong federal government and closer ties with Great Britain. The Democratic-Republicans wanted limits on federal power and a closer relationship with France. These disagreements continued in the early 1800s. However, the Democratic-Republicans grew stronger, and the Federalists faded away. After the War of 1812, during James Monroe's presidency, the nation saw relative political unity for the first time in its young history.

When partisanship returned in the 1820s, it was within the Democratic-Republican Party itself. Four candidates ran to replace Monroe, causing the party to split. Those who favored states' rights, including the right to practice slavery, formed the Democratic Party. It unified around Andrew Jackson, who won the U.S. presidency in 1828 and 1832. The subgroup that favored a strong federal government and were less supportive of slavery formed the Whig Party. Whig William Henry Harrison won the 1840 election.

While the Democratic Party began in the 1820s with Jackson, the Republican Party took longer to form. The addition of new

John Adams (*center*) and Thomas Jefferson (*right*) faced off in the country's first partisan election in 1796.

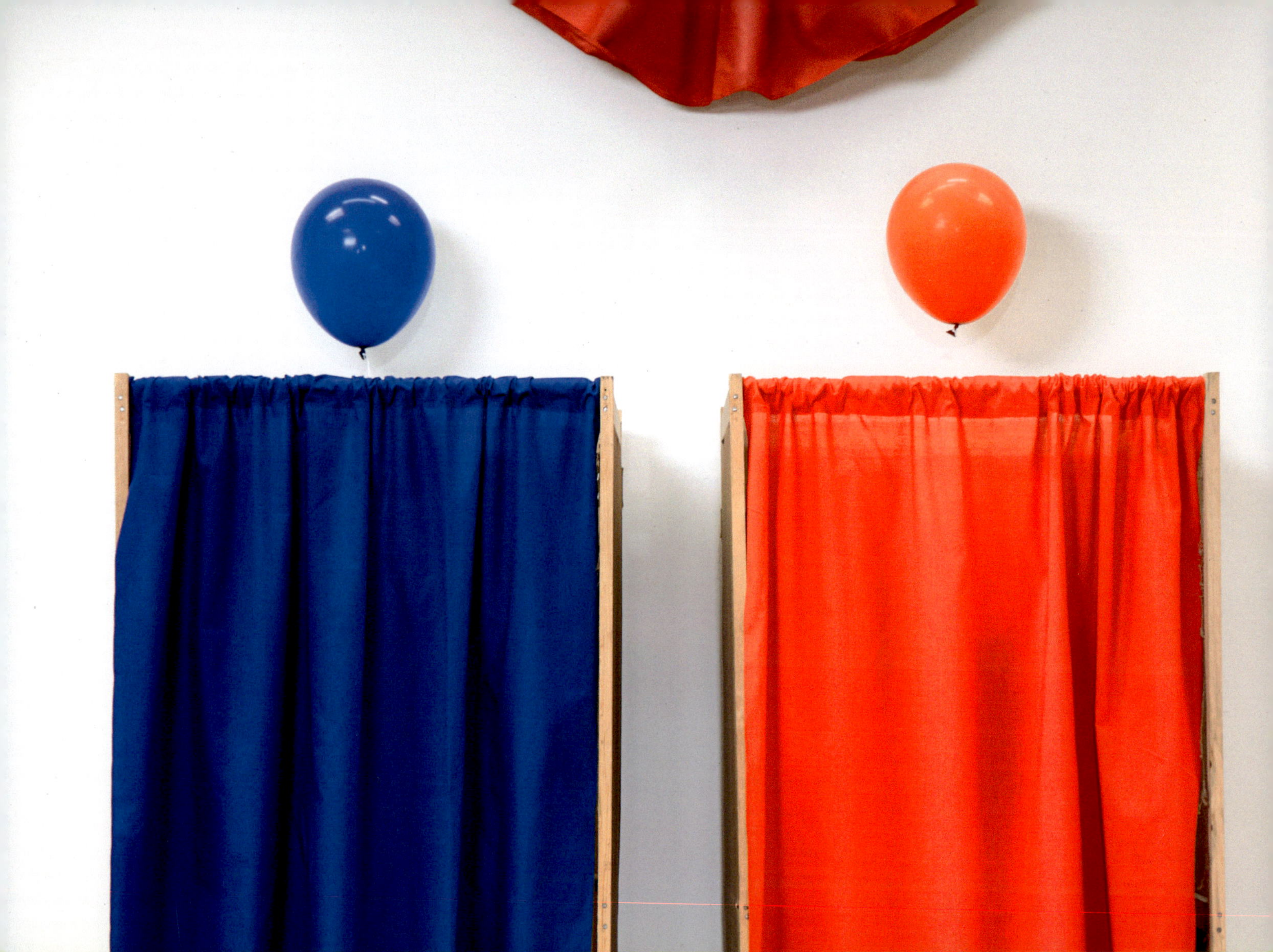

ZOOM IN: WINNER TAKES ALL

The U.S. political system makes it difficult for a third party to enter the government arena. The main reason is that the system is based on the principle of "winner takes all." For example, a candidate for Congress only needs to win more than half the votes in their district to get elected. In other countries, if a party gets 10 percent of all the votes, it gets 10 percent of all the seats. In the United States, there is no prize for getting less than 50 percent. This rule keeps out candidates from smaller parties.

territory after the Mexican-American War (1846–48) fueled the debate over slavery. People argued whether the new territories should have slaves or not. Supporters of slavery won victories with the Compromise of 1850 and the Kansas-Nebraska Act. Opponents of slavery, including Whigs, reacted by forming the Republican Party in 1854.

In 1854, Democrats and Republicans faced off for the first time in a presidential election. Disagreement between the parties was strong, mostly over the expansion of slavery. Democrat James Buchanan narrowly won the presidency, but he did not run for a second term. Helped by a split in the Democratic Party, Republican Abraham Lincoln won the presidency in 1860. Southern states, which had refused to put Lincoln on the ballot, broke away from the Northern states in protest and became the Confederacy. The Civil War (1861–65) began just months later.

The Union's victory in the Civil War made the Republican Party the major power in national politics. During Reconstruction (1865–77) and the Gilded Age (1877–96), Republican administrations favored a strong federal government and support for big business. The government gave land to railroads and funded the construction of the Transcontinental Railroad. Other changes were the constitutional amendments that tried to achieve equality for African Americans. They guaranteed citizenship to former enslaved people and gave African American men the right to vote. In reaction, the South supported Democrats.

In the Compromise of 1877, Southern states agreed to give their votes to Republican presidential candidate Rutherford B.

For many voters, the choice is either blue (Democrat) or red (Republican).

Hayes in exchange for the withdrawal of Union troops from the South. The move ended Reconstruction, the era when the federal government tried to reform the Southern states. As a result, African American equality was largely eliminated as a major goal of the Republican Party.

The Gilded Age was good for big business but not for farmers and the working class. Farmers in the South and West struggled because of low crop prices and high shipping rates. **Populists**, who called for policies in support of working-class people, gained ground. They merged into the Democratic Party. Some of them were **Progressives** who wanted the government to be more involved in the **economy**.

The Progressives wanted government control, or regulation, of railroads, banks, and big business. Progressive William Jennings Bryan was the Democratic choice for the presidency in 1896, 1900, and 1908. He campaigned, which was rare at that time. For this reason, he is considered the first modern candidate. He helped change the image of the Democratic Party from Southern and rural to pro-labor (standing up for workers).

The Democratic Party grew stronger but not enough to displace the Republicans. Republican president Theodore Roosevelt served two terms, from 1901 to 1909. He came back to challenge his successor, William Howard Taft, for his party's support to run again. After he failed to gain this support, he formed his own Bull Moose Party. By doing so, Roosevelt split the Republican vote, and Democrat Woodrow Wilson won the White House in 1912. Wilson was a university professor who gave the Democratic Party a more urban feel. He continued Progressive reforms, such as

U.S. president Franklin Delano Roosevelt held office from 1933 until his death in 1945.

more rights for workers and women. But he was also a Southerner opposed to racial equality.

Republicans returned to power after Wilson's second term ended in 1920. But the Great Depression (1929–39) turned Americans against their pro-big business policies. It helped Democrat Franklin Delano Roosevelt (FDR) win the White House in 1932. FDR promised federal intervention in the economy to end the depression. His policies are known as the "New Deal."

The Roosevelt administration poured federal money into big projects that gave jobs to the unemployed. These projects were run by new federal agencies. FDR also started major social programs such as Social Security. His policies were so popular that he won a record four presidential terms. The Democratic Party became

U.S. president Lyndon B. Johnson shakes the hand of civil rights leader Martin Luther King, Jr. before signing the Civil Rights Act of 1964.

linked with the regulation of industries. The New Deal, and World War II (1939–45), expanded the federal government.

Because of the New Deal, Democrats dominated national politics, and they remained united through the Great Depression and World War II. However, the federal government's expansion, the increased number of African Americans joining the party, and the party's growing support for civil rights alarmed Southern Democrats.

The Southern Democrats split off into the Dixiecrat Party, or States' Rights Democrats. They put up their own presidential candidate, Strom Thurmond, in 1948. He was not successful, but Southern Democrats remained at odds with the rest of the Democratic Party.

President John F. Kennedy, a Democrat, supported minority rights. When he was assassinated in 1963, his successor, Lyndon B. Johnson, helped push the Civil Rights Act of 1964 through Congress. The law ended racial **discrimination** in hiring practices and school **segregation**. The Voting Rights Act of 1965 ended discriminatory voting practices adopted in the South after the Civil War. Many Southern Democrats were outraged and left the party.

In 1968, former Democrat George Wallace ran for the U.S. presidency as an Independent. He built his message around "law and order," which appealed to segregationists. He did not win. But he developed a strong following among rural white Southerners and **blue-collar** workers in the North. The Republican Party adopted Wallace's law-and-order message. The Southern Democrats who had left the party joined the Republicans led by Richard Nixon.

ZOOM IN: THE GREATEST DIVIDE

No issue has divided American society along more bitter lines than slavery. The debate over slavery, and whether it should be allowed to spread into new territories beyond the South and border states, eventually led to the Civil War (1861–65). Between Abraham Lincoln's election in 1860 and Robert E. Lee's surrender in 1865, the nation literally broke apart. More than three million people took up arms, and hundreds of thousands of civilians became refugees. Between 620,000 and 750,000 people died. After the war ended, the nation entered a heated and sometimes violent debate on how to move forward in the absence of slavery.

The election of Barack Obama to the U.S. presidency in 2008 polarized the two major political parties.

In 1980, Ronald Reagan won the Republican presidential nomination. He criticized the growth of the federal government, high taxes, and weak foreign policy. He called for stronger national defense. He also joined forces with the New Right, a movement of religious people who stood for "traditional values."

As a result of all the shifts in beliefs between 1860 and 1980, the two major political parties in the United States had largely switched sides. The Republicans, who had started out socially liberal and urban, became socially conservative and rural. The Democrats, who had started out socially conservative and rural, became socially liberal and urban.

In the early 1990s, the two parties' agendas were more similar than they are today. Since then, they have drifted apart, becoming more polarized. Democrats nominated the first non-white presidential candidate, Barack Obama. The Democratic-controlled Congress passed the Affordable Care Act (Obamacare). The biggest health care reform since the creation of Medicare in 1965, it placed regulations on health care insurance companies. Conservatives reacted to these developments by starting the Tea Party movement. The Tea Party sought to repeal Obamacare and to reduce the power of the federal government overall.

In 2016, many blue-collar workers and labor groups (unions) swung away from the Democratic Party, leading to the election of President Donald Trump. Some analysts believe it was in reaction to Democrats' support for urban, high-tech industries, rather than traditional manufacturing. Trump commanded both strong loyalty and extreme resentment. When he lost the presidency to Democrat Joe Biden in 2020, his supporters stormed the U.S. Capitol, hoping to overturn the results of the election.

CHAPTER 2:

Polarizing Forces

In general, Democrats are associated with the labels "left" and "liberal." They favor social and economic policies that expand the social safety net. Examples of such policies include keeping abortion legal, allowing **LGBTQ+** people to marry, expanding government-provided health care, and increasing the minimum wage.

The Democratic Party tends to support unions and minorities. It supports higher taxes, especially on the wealthy, to fund social programs. It favors more gun control and paths to citizenship for immigrants.

Republicans are generally associated with the labels "right" and "conservative." Economically, this means lowering taxes and limiting government regulation of businesses. Examples of social policies include limiting access to abortion, ending race-based college admissions, supporting gun rights, and restricting immigration.

By the early 21st century, many analysts had also adopted the labels "red state" and "blue state." Red is the color for Republicans and blue for Democrats. Red states are generally in the South,

Blue states voted Democrat in all presidential elections from 2008 to 2020, while red ones voted Republican. Other states fluctuated.

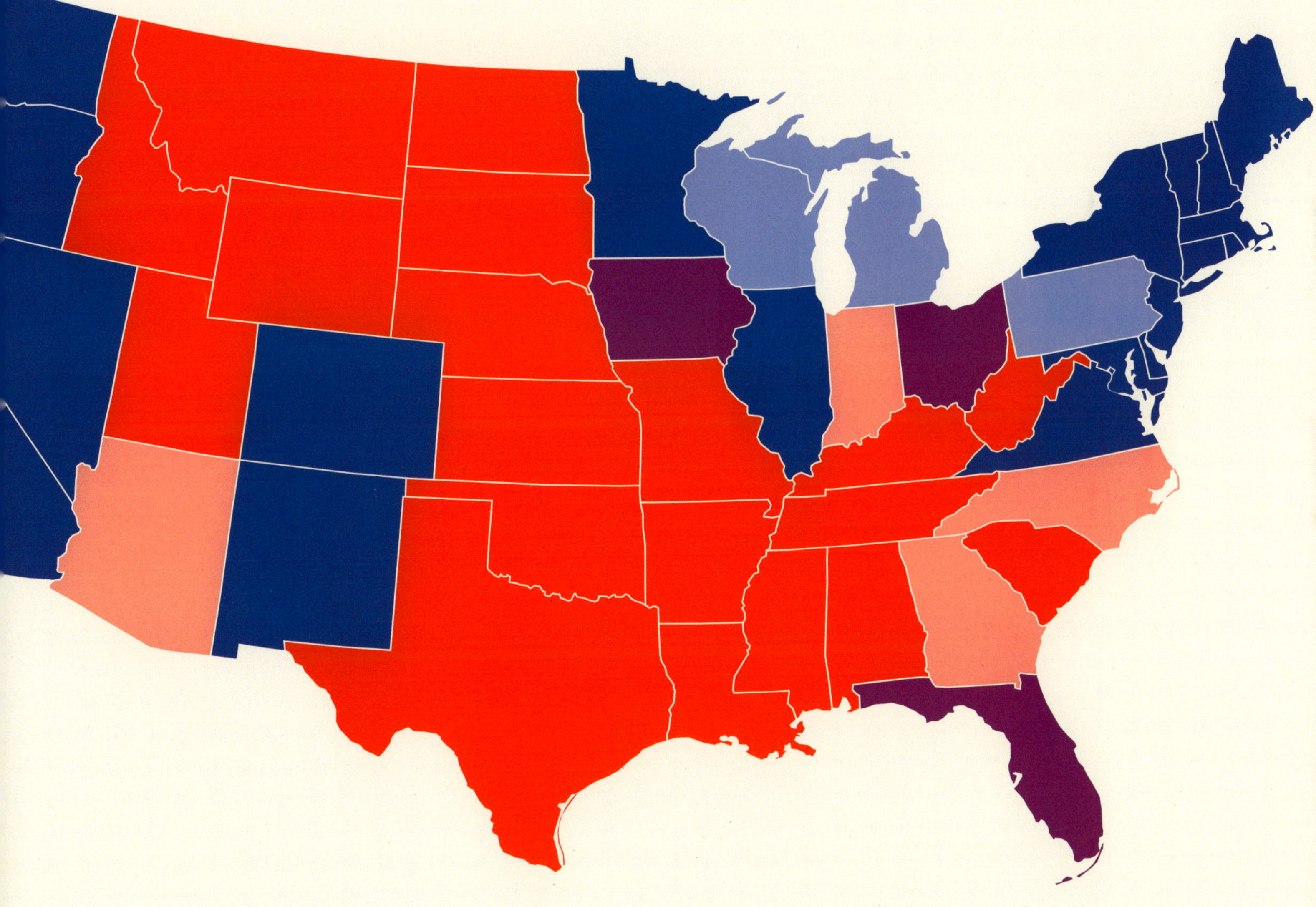

West, and Lower Midwest. They are Republican, conservative, small-town or suburban, religious, pro-life (against abortion), and against same-sex marriage. Blue states are mostly in the Northeast, Upper Midwest, and West Coast. They are Democratic, liberal, urban, non-faith-based, pro-choice (in favor of keeping abortion legal), and in favor of same-sex marriage. Regional differences exist, too. For example, Democrats in the South are usually more conservative than Democrats in the Northeast and on the West Coast. Republicans in the Northeast usually have more liberal views than Republicans in the South or the mountain states in the West.

Political scientists say they can guess a person's political "home" with just a few questions. Support gun control and environmental protections? Democrat. Concerned about immigration and strengthening the military? Republican.

A Pew Research Center survey conducted in June 2023 found wide differences in how Democrats and Republicans prioritized national problems. Inflation was the top concern for Republicans and Republican-leaning Independents, with 77 percent saying it was a very big problem. The state of moral values, illegal immigration, and the budget deficit also were seen as top problems by at

ZOOM IN: VOTING BY ADDRESS

People in the United States tend to live among their own kind—those who look, think, and live like them. Experts say it is increasingly possible to determine how a person may vote based on where they live. Cities have long favored Democrats, but the gap has become wider. In 2018, 62 percent of urban voters identified as Democrat, and 31 percent identified as Republican. In 1997, the ratio was 55 to 37 percent, according to the Pew Research Center. Rural voters favored Democrats by a 45-44 margin in 1997. By 2018, this had flipped, with voters favoring Republicans 54-38.

The use of mail-in ballots is another gap between parties, with Democrats generally *for* and Republicans *against*.

least two-thirds of Republicans. For Democrats and Democratic leaners, gun violence was the top concern. About 8 out of 10 people (81 percent) said it was a very big problem. The affordability of health care ranked second (73 percent).

Gaps between the two parties were significant when asked about the environment and immigration. Democrats were more than four times as likely as Republicans to say that climate change was a big concern in the country (64 percent versus 14 percent). Republicans were more than twice as likely as Democrats to say that illegal immigration was a big one (70 percent versus 25 percent).

According to the survey, the U.S. public, as a whole, agreed with the Democratic Party on policies related to abortion, health care, and climate change. However, the Republican Party held a 12-point advantage on economic policy: 42 percent of all Americans said they agreed with it, while 30 percent said they agreed with the economic policies of the Democratic Party. Republicans held similar leads on crime and immigration.

Some people say Americans today are more divided than ever before. But many historians disagree. They point out examples of large divisions throughout the country's history. Case in point: Americans were so at odds over slavery that they broke apart a nation and fought a civil war that killed 2 percent of the population! Each historic period has had its own kinds of divisions, including economic, social, racial, gender, and political. In the 20th century, the Great Depression saw divisions about economic policy. The civil rights movement of the 1960s was a time of high racial tensions. The Vietnam War (1955–75) split society on foreign policy and military interventions.

Although it can lead to gridlock and inaction, having different ideas on issues is not necessarily bad. That is how democracy works. It provides people with choice. The clash of opinions can help find the truth. Some people even argue that too much compromise and agreement can hurt. For example, in 1877, compromise came at the expense of African Americans, who lost their constitutional rights in exchange for settling a presidential election dispute. In 1950, some political scientists worried that national politics was too bland, that voters cared only about local issues. They thought it would be better to have *more* disagreement.

But there is a kind of division that scholars do consider dangerous. Some call it "belief polarization" or "group polarization." Others prefer the term "affective polarization." This type of division turns people into more extreme versions of themselves. They become overly confident and more willing to engage in risky behaviors. Belief polarization leads people to embrace negative feelings about those

Donald Trump is often accused of inciting intolerance and aggression in his supporters.

ZOOM IN: DIVIDED ON ABORTION

In 1973, *Roe v. Wade* guaranteed a constitutional right to an abortion in the United States. In June 2022, the U.S. Supreme Court overturned the ruling and gave individual states the authority to set their own abortion policies. According to the Pew Research Center, 57 percent of Americans disapproved of overturning *Roe*, while 41 percent approved. Abortion has always been a hot topic, and Republicans and Democrats were sharply divided in their views. Eighty-two percent of Democrats and Democratic-leaning Independents disapproved of the 2022 decision. Seventy percent of Republicans and Republican leaners approved.

with different views. As they shift toward extremism, they define themselves and others primarily as opponents, or partisans. Eventually, politics expands beyond policy ideas and into entire lifestyles.

Partisanship has seeped into every aspect of American life. Even things that do not appear political carry partisan messages. For example, a 2018 study found that conservatives and liberals decorate their homes differently. In general, conservatives like flags and clocks, while liberals like maps and art. Camouflage clothes are often associated with conservatives and yoga pants with liberals. Liberals buy their coffee at Starbucks, conservatives at Dunkin'. Conservatives watch stock car racing, while liberals watch arthouse movies. Someone who posts a photo of a hunting trip on social media is assumed to be a Republican. Someone who posts a picture of a farmers market is assumed to be a Democrat.

Each political group deeply misperceives the other. For example, Republicans estimate that 32 percent of Democrats are LGBTQ+, when the actual number is 6 percent. Democrats estimate that 38 percent of Republicans earn more than $250,000 per year, when the actual number is only 2 percent.

Protesters urge lawmakers to allow accessible, safe, affordable abortion services to all Americans.

The Washington Monument, honoring first U.S. president George Washington, towers above the nation's capital.

People in the United States have become more invested in policing the boundaries between "us" and "them." For example, one study found that in 1960, only 4 percent of Republicans and 4 percent of Democrats said they would be displeased if their child married someone of the opposite party. In 2019, 45 percent of Democrats and 35 percent of Republicans said so.

Some scholars talk about how polarization leads people to go beyond mistrusting the other side. It pushes them to feel contempt for it and see it as less moral, evil, or as an "existential threat." Experts call this "tribalism" or "sectarianism" and compare it to the divisions that have historically separated religious groups. Political identity then becomes like a religious identity.

Sectarianism has three ingredients. One is "othering," the tendency to see opponents as very different from oneself. The second is "aversion," intense dislike or distrust. The third is "moralization," the idea that opponents are wicked or even criminal.

The combination of these ingredients is what makes sectarianism dangerous. If two partisans basically trust each other, they could still solve policy differences through compromise or persuasion. But if they see each other as a moral threat, it becomes a zero-sum game. In response to the "existential threat" posed by the other side, partisans may even excuse or justify anti-democratic behaviors. They may, for example, violate election laws, oppose checks and balances, and promote unrest.

As people focus on hostility toward those who disagree with them, they become more intolerant, even of allies. They become less able to navigate disagreement. They come to believe democracy is possible only if everyone agrees with them. This, in fact, is a very *undemocratic* point of view.

CHAPTER 3:

Deepening Divisions

Polarization is complex. Scholars are still trying to determine why divisions are deepening. Some blame the increased influence of political activists.

Activists push for policies that are further to the left (in the Democratic Party) or to the right (in the Republican Party). This push widens the gap between the two party platforms. Recent policy changes have made it easier for activists to affect elections. Changes in campaign finance rules have enabled them to give large amounts of money to candidates of their choice.

Special-interest groups have encouraged divisions to advance their agendas, or for profit. The Southern Poverty Law Center has identified at least 1,000 hate groups in the United States. Many of these groups have used race and anti-immigration feelings to divide people. **Conspiracy** theory groups such as QAnon have spread misinformation and even become part of conservative politics.

TRUMP
-2020-
KEEP AMERICA GREAT!
TRUMP
CERTIFY

ZOOM IN: QANON

QAnon is a set of Internet conspiracy theories. They claim the world is run by a secret group of Satan-worshiping people who have sex with children and then eat them. This group is said to include top Democrats, Hollywood stars, and religious figures. According to QAnon, top generals urged Donald Trump to run for president in 2016 to break up this criminal ring and bring its members to justice. In 2020, QAnon supporters flooded social media with false information about COVID-19, the Black Lives Matter protests, and the presidential election. Some believers participated in the 2021 Capitol riot and have been charged with violent crimes.

Primary elections also push the parties further apart. In primaries, members of the same party choose which candidate will represent that party in the general election. Most people don't vote in primaries, but activists do. To appeal to these activists, the candidates adopt more extreme positions.

In addition, many voting districts have been gerrymandered. Gerrymandering is the practice of drawing the boundaries of a district in a way that gives one party an advantage over the other. Some districts are overwhelmingly populated by members of the same party. Gerrymandered districts often elect candidates who appeal to the party's faithful, not to those in the middle.

Another factor is "in-group **bias**." People may think they form opinions by rationally reviewing policies. But research finds otherwise. Once people join a group, they often change their political opinions to match the group.

Many Americans are exposed to partisan news in their social media feeds. Online platforms such as YouTube, Facebook, Twitter, and others use algorithms. These formulas direct users to content that reinforces the users' world view. The algorithms promote posts that use extremist language to increase "engagement." Users get

ZOOM IN: BARACK OBAMA

The presidency of Barack Obama highlighted the expanding division in the United States. During Obama's first year in office, 88 percent of Democrats, but only 23 percent of Republicans, approved of how he did his job. That's a difference of 65 percent. What was so controversial about him? The first Black president, from a mixed-race background, had to deal with deeply entrenched racism. He also faced a growing economic inequality in the country and a Republican Congress that would compromise on almost nothing. Obama's support for an overhaul of the country's health care system, called Obamacare, made him a target of constant attacks.

exposed to extreme content without realizing it. Spending time in these political "eco chambers" can make it easier to develop negative feelings toward people on the other side of the political fence. Users hear only opinions they already agree with. They see stories that align with their world view. As a result, they may become more immoveable in their beliefs, whether their beliefs reflect the real world or not. They may also become easier to manipulate and more extreme.

Scholars say that "media bubbles" did not form overnight. In the 1980s, the Reagan administration took steps to reduce government controls on industries. As part of this effort, it ended "the fairness doctrine" in broadcasting. The doctrine had been put in place after World War II. It required news media to present opposing viewpoints. Once this rule was gone, partisans started outlets such as Fox News, CNN, and MSNBC.

Social media and the rise of cable TV news networks are often blamed for the increase in political polarization. However, some experts believe they are not causes but rather outlets through which partisan debate spreads. Fox News provided a TV platform for conservative voices, but those voices were already on talk radio, for example. Cable news networks and social media platforms do well because people like what they see, hear, and share. Their views are affirmed, and they feel part of a like-minded community. This phenomenon is known as "confirmation bias."

While social media may not be driving polarization, it does make it more visible. And it makes dividing people easier. People are more likely to say something negative on social media than in person. There are no immediate consequences for someone behind a computer or smartphone screen. The most significant impact of this visibility and ease is on moderates. When partisans promote aggressive politics on social media, moderates may be turned off. This hurts the chances for compromise, as moderates may be in the best position to bridge the gap between the two major parties.

Some scholars look beyond elections and the media for the source of growing polarization. They point to features of American society that they say politicians have long ignored. They blame the nation's troubled history of race relations and the very nature of the U.S. economic system.

The United States has been slow in addressing the legacy of racism. It took almost a century after the end of the Civil War to pass the Civil Rights Act. Steps were taken in more recent decades to address more of this legacy. For example, anti-discrimination laws were put in place. Race was considered in college admissions (a policy recently struck down by the Supreme Court). But many Americans see the work as unfinished, as shown by race riots.

Division led to the Civil War and its bloodiest battle, Gettysburg—three days in which 51,000 people died, were wounded, or went missing.

ZOOM IN: THE MONEY DIVIDE

The highest-earning 20 percent of U.S. households take a larger share of the country's overall income than they did 40 years ago. The gap between the richest and poorest families has more than doubled. Millennials are far less likely than baby boomers to earn more than their parents did. Economic equality is still out of reach for households of color and women. The incomes of white Americans are consistently around twice those of Blacks and Hispanics.

On the other side of the coin, some white Americans (many of them rural) feel threatened by the rising number and influence of people of color. This anxiety has some economic roots, but it is also seen in racial terms. Racial resentment may be behind efforts to redraw maps of voting districts and make voting more difficult in non-white neighborhoods.

Polarization is part of the country's economic system. American-style capitalism rewards risk-taking and new ideas, and it produces huge wealth. But it also leaves U.S. workers with a weaker social safety net than workers in other developed countries. Thirty years ago, when people talked about workers in trouble, they usually meant blue-collar workers whose jobs were moved overseas. Now, automation and artificial intelligence are also gradually displacing a wider set of workers. This is a concern for people on the right *and* left. The result is voters who are more worried about the future and more susceptible to populist politicians.

These and other trends feed off of and reinforce each other. High economic insecurity is linked to a rise in hate crimes. Mistrust of the government leads to the election of outsider candidates. In turn, these outsiders lash out against traditional politicians and institutions, further damaging people's trust in the system.

CHAPTER 4:

Building Bridges

Police officers engage with community members to build trust and open lines of communication.

Bridging deep divisions and mistrust is difficult. Some analysts go as far as suggesting that it won't happen until younger voters replace older generations.

Millennials and Gen Z voters (voters under the age of 40) are more agreeable on some of the cultural ideas that divide older Americans. As a group, they tend to be more supportive of climate change and LGBTQ+ rights, for example.

Healing the divisions could start with the electoral process itself. Campaign finance reform may help, by ending huge contributions from the most extreme donors. One idea is to finance elections entirely with public funds. Another idea is to open up primaries. If anyone could vote in a party primary, the candidates would be less likely to serve the biggest partisans. Fixing partisan gerrymandering could also encourage more competition in elections.

Not all eligible voters in the United States vote, even in general elections. People who feel very strongly about politics are the most likely to vote, so they have an outsized influence on the national agenda. One way to change this is by increasing

POLICE
T.B. COX
6497

voter turnout. Some countries, such as Australia, have made voting mandatory. The United States could follow this example.

Offering a choice beyond "left" and "right" could break up the power of the two-party system. Some cities, for example, have instant-runoff or ranked-choice voting. In ranked-choice voting, voters rank the candidates in order of preference. If their top choice does not get enough votes, the vote goes to their next choice. The candidate with the least votes is eliminated. This process goes on until the top vote-getters win, regardless of which party they belong to.

A big question is what to do about social media. Experts are divided on how to encourage people to spend more time checking the truth of claims on Facebook or Twitter. One strategy is to rely on **crowdsourcing** to identify accurate content. The hope is to reduce the spread of false or hyper-partisan posts and memes. Tech companies could re-write algorithms so these platforms would be less likely to make people extreme in the first place. Another way is by educating people on how to best use social media.

Several attempts to help social media users escape their echo chambers have started in recent years. One of them is FlipFeed. This plug-in allows users to replace their own Twitter feeds with those of random strangers. Another is Escape Your Bubble. This plug-in inserts opposing political views into users' Facebook newsfeeds. Experts urge people to follow a variety of news sources that examine issues from different political angles. Websites such as AllSides can help people find out more about the political leanings of different news outlets.

ZOOM IN: CRITICAL RACE THEORY

Liberals see the issue of critical race theory (CRT) as a way to understand how racism has shaped public policy. Conservatives say it sets groups against one another. According to CRT, racism is not just the product of individual prejudice, but it is also embedded in legal systems and policies. For example, CRT supporters quote housing policies in the 1930s. The government drew lines around areas considered poor financial risks, often because that is where Black people lived. Banks then refused to offer mortgages to Black people in these areas. Conservatives, however, say CRT divides people by focusing on group, rather than universal, values. It labels them either "oppressors" or "oppressed" and promotes intolerance.

Studies find that Americans are less likely to express negative feelings toward someone if they are told that the other person doesn't care about politics. It is helpful to focus on things that people have in common. These things may include their shared identity as Americans or as fans of the same sports teams or TV shows.

Learning to focus on policy details, rather than identity groups, may help people appreciate others and become humbler. People could decide which policies they want to pass, not which political party they want to win. Getting involved in local politics is a good idea, too. At that level, issues often matter more than parties.

Not all policies are divisive, either. Many of them have support from both liberals and conservatives. For example, 78 percent of Americans are in favor of encouraging highly skilled immigrants to come to the United States. Sixty percent support public spending to weatherize homes to make them more energy efficient. Eighty-five percent are in favor of requiring background checks on people who buy guns through private sales or gun shows.

Correcting misperceptions about others may help reduce hostility and narrow the divide. Psychologists say there is evidence that when people are made aware of their biases, they are less likely to give in to them. Try to understand where people on the other side of the divide are coming from. Don't rush to judgment. Learn to listen and listen to learn.

Getting Real

DONALD TRUMP

Donald Trump, the 45th president of the United States, was one of the most divisive presidents in U.S. history. His critics say he helped deepen mistrust of the government, media, and other institutions. His fiercely loyal supporters say he "made America great again."

Trump won the 2016 presidential election by appealing largely to rural voters and blue-collar workers whose jobs got "shipped" overseas. He promised to reverse their fortunes and bring those jobs back home.

Trump pursued controversial immigration policies. He imposed a travel ban on people from several Muslim countries. He also called Mexican immigrants "drug dealers, criminals, and rapists." Trump promised to build a wall along the U.S. border with Mexico. His supporters say he helped discourage unauthorized immigration and protected the nation's citizens. Trump also withdrew the United States from various international commitments.

Trump's presidency overlapped with the COVID-19 pandemic. The global event split the nation on issues such as mask wearing, vaccines, and lockdowns. Trump initially downplayed the pandemic and refused to wear a mask.

When Trump lost the 2020 election to Democrat Joe Biden, he promoted a proven falsehood, that the election was "stolen." Trump loyalists stormed the U.S. Capitol to try to reverse the outcome of the election. Several people died.

Trump is the only president to be charged with misconduct, or impeached, twice: once for abuse of power in his dealings with Ukraine and once for fueling the Capitol riots.

RICHARD NIXON

Richard Nixon, the 37th U.S. president, is the only president ever to resign from office. Nixon stepped down halfway through his second term, on August 9, 1974. He did so rather than face misconduct charges over his efforts to cover up illegal activities in the Watergate scandal.

The Watergate scandal began in the early morning of June 17, 1972. Several burglars were arrested in the office of the Democratic National Committee, in the Watergate complex of buildings in Washington, D.C. But this was no ordinary robbery. The prowlers were connected to Nixon's reelection campaign. They had been caught wiretapping phones and stealing documents. Nixon took great steps to cover up the crimes. When reporters revealed Nixon's role in the conspiracy, he resigned.

Even before Watergate, Nixon had troubles. His paranoid personal style resulted in numerous abuses of power. These included using the Federal Bureau of Investigation (FBI) to wiretap 17 government officials and journalists.

The scandals overshadowed some of the achievements of the Nixon administration. Nixon helped create the Environmental Protection Agency and passed the Endangered Species Act and the Clean Air Act. His visit to China in 1972 led to diplomatic relations between the two nations. He also concluded the Anti-Ballistic Missile Treaty with the Soviet Union. Nixon ended U.S. involvement in the Vietnam conflict and the military draft in 1973.

However, Nixon's involvement in Watergate tarnished his legacy and deepened Americans' distrust of the government. The Watergate scandal has been called the gold standard of American political scandals.

Timeline

1787
The Founding Fathers draw up a new constitution for the United States of America.

1789
George Washington is elected as the first U.S. president.

1796
Federalist John Adams defeats Democratic-Republican Thomas Jefferson in the first partisan presidential election.

1800
Jefferson defeats Adams, resulting in the first transfer of power between parties.

1854
Opponents of slavery set up the Republican Party; Democrats and Republicans face off for the first time.

1860-61
Eleven pro-slavery states break away from the Union, triggering civil war between the North and the South.

1877
The Compromise of 1877 trades votes for the withdrawal of Union troops from the South.

1896
Democratic presidential nominee William Jennings Bryan becomes the first modern candidate.

1911
Former Republican president Theodore Roosevelt forms the Bull Moose Party and splits the Republican vote.

1933
President Franklin Delano Roosevelt launches the "New Deal" recovery program.

1948
Southern Democrats split off into the Dixiecrat Party and put up their own presidential candidate.

1964
The Civil Rights Act is signed into law.

1968
George Wallace runs for the presidency as an Independent, appealing to supporters of segregation.

1974
President Nixon resigns due to the Watergate scandal.

2008
Democrat Barack Obama becomes the first Black president.

2010
Democrats in Congress pass a health care reform bill, despite Republican opposition.

2020
Nationwide protests break out following the killing of George Floyd by police.

2021
Joe Biden assumes the presidency, one week after Trump supporters storm the U.S. Capitol.

Glossary

bias—being for or against an idea, person, or group, usually in an unfair way

blue-collar—relating to manual work, especially in manufacturing

conservative—supportive of policies favoring free enterprise, private ownership, and socially traditional ideas

conspiracy—a secret plan by a group to do something unlawful or harmful

crowdsourcing—obtaining information by enlisting the services of a large number of people, usually on the Internet

discrimination—applying different treatment to someone based on factors other than individual merit, such as race, gender, or income

economy—the goods and services produced by a country or region

LGBTQ+—an abbreviation for lesbian, gay, bisexual, transgender, queer, and other people of "non-traditional" gender

liberal—supportive of policies that promote social welfare

partisanship—strong support for a party

polarize—to break into opposing groups

populist—a politician who tries to appeal to ordinary people who feel that their concerns are not heard

Progressive—a politician who supports reform and new ideas

ratify—to make official

segregation—being kept apart, usually based on race or class

Selected Bibliography

Campbell, James E. *Polarized: Making Sense of a Divided America.* Princeton, N.J.: Princeton University Press, 2016.

Chua, Amy. *Political Tribes: Group Instinct and the Fate of Nations.* New York: Penguin Press, 2018.

Grinspan, Jon. *The Age of Acrimony: How Americans Fought to Fix Their Democracy, 1865–1915.* New York: Bloomsbury Publishing, 2021.

Kettl, Donald F. *The Divided States of America: Why Federalism Doesn't Work.* Princeton, N.J.: Princeton University Press, 2020.

Klein, Ezra. *Why We're Polarized.* New York: Avid Reader Press, 2020.

Mettler, Suzanne, and Robert C. Lieberman. *Four Threats: The Recurring Crises of American Democracy.* New York: St. Martin's Press, 2020.

Settle, Jaime E. *Frenemies: How Social Media Polarizes America.* Cambridge; New York: Cambridge University Press, 2018.

Talisse, Robert B. *Sustaining Democracy: What We Owe to the Other Side.* New York: Oxford University Press, 2021.

Websites

Cornell University: Department of Government

https://government.cornell.edu/news/exploring-widening-chasm-between-urban-and-rural-voters

Read about the gap between U.S. voters in urban and rural areas.

PBS Learning Media: U.S. History Collection

https://tpt.pbslearningmedia org/resource/ush22-soc-politicalparties/political-division-early-america/?student=true

An interactive lesson on the rise of political division in the United States.

Pew Research Center

https://www.pewresearch.org/topic/politics-policy/political-parties-polarization

Explore facts and trends regarding U.S. political parties and polarization.

Index